the temper tantrum book

the temper tantrum book

Edna Mitchell Preston

Illustrated by Rainey Bennett

SCHOLASTIC INC.
New York Toronto London Auckland Sydney

ISBN 0-590-36220-8

Text copyright © 1969 by Edna Mitchell Preston. Illustrations copyright © 1969 by Rainey Bennett. This edition published by Scholastic Inc., 730 Broadway, New York, NY 10003, by arrangement with Viking Penguin Inc.

12   4 5 6 7/9

Printed in the U.S.A.   08

What is bothering Lionel Lion?

Why is he hopping around?

Why is he roaring and raging and crying?

Why is he stomping the ground?

I hate it

when you comb my hair when it has tangles in it.

What is annoying Elizabeth Elephant

Under that nice cool shower?

Why is she kicking and hitting and howling

And screaming with all her power?

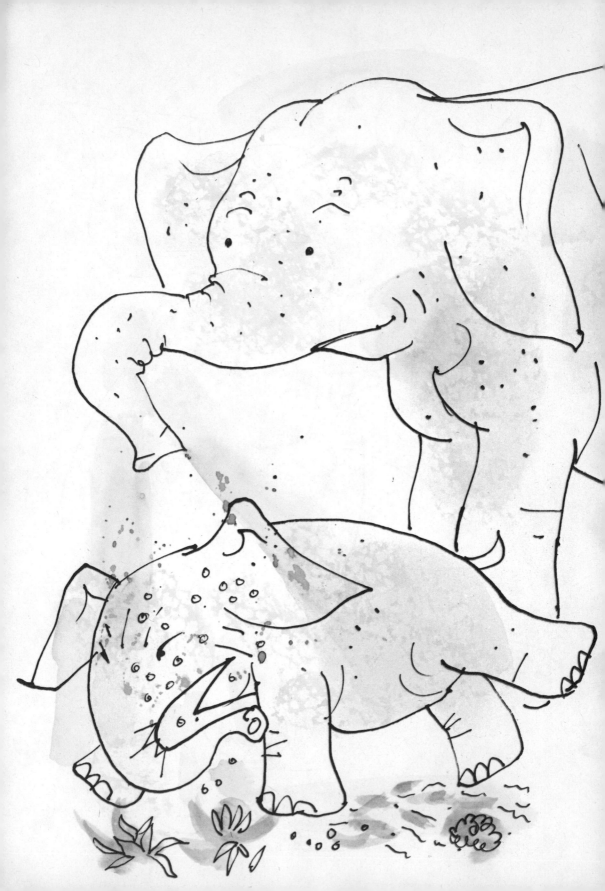

I hate it

when you get soap in my eyes.

What can be causing Persnickety Piggery

To put on that miserable pout?

Why is he squealing and snorting and scowling?

What is he shouting about?

I hate it

when you give him a bigger piece than me.

I should get the most because I like it the most.

What is infuriating Terrible Turtle?

Why is he fussing so?

Why is he throwing a temper tantrum?

Where does he want to go?

I hate it

when you say I have to stay in.

And it's not even raining hard. I won't get wet. Honest.

What is exasperating Cathaleen Kangaroo

Making her glower and frown?

Why is she making disagreeable faces

Squinching her eyebrows down?

I hate it

when you make me stay still and not wiggle.

I *like* to flop around and put my feet up.

What is perturbing Olivia Otter?

Why is she making a row?

Why is she flipping and flapping

and floundering?

What is disturbing her now?

I hate it

when you make me stop playing

and I'm not through yet.

Why do I have to come in and
take a nap and nobody else has to.

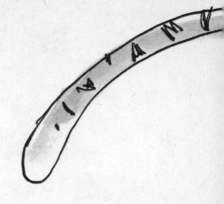

What is maddening Thomas Q. Tiger

Splitting the air with his yowls?

Why is he bawling bloodcurdling bellows?

Why is he growling growls?

I hate it

when you wash my face and rub too hard.

What can be pleasuring Henrietta Hippopotamus?

Why is she smirking so brightly?

What can be setting Henrietta to twirling

And whirling about so lightly?

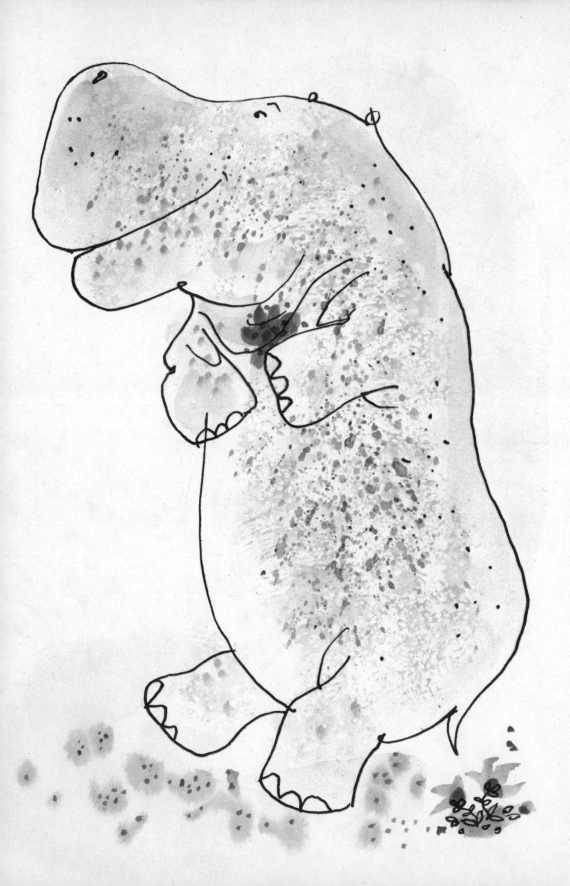

I love it

when you let me play in the mud.